RAPPACCINI'S DAUGHTER

SILVER EDITION

NATHANIEL HAWTHORNE

EDITED BY
ADAPTIVE READER

CONTENTS

INTRODUCTION

Welcome to Adaptive Reader, your portal to the captivating world of literature, tailored to fit your unique reading abilities.

In today's fast-paced and diverse learning environment, we believe in the power of personalized learning experiences. That's where the concept of leveled reading comes in, and why we, at Adaptive Reader, have dedicated ourselves to offering a broad collection of classic novels at various reading levels. Our mission is to make the joy and benefits of reading accessible to everyone.

THE BENEFITS OF LEVELED TEXTS

So, what exactly is leveled reading? It's an approach that matches students with texts that align with their unique reading abilities. This ensures that every reader is challenged just the right amount - enough to grow, but not so much that they feel overwhelmed or frustrated.

For students, this means you'll engage with texts that stretch your reading skills while keeping the experience enjoyable and manageable. You'll gain confidence as you successfully comprehend each level and feel motivated to explore more challenging texts as your reading skills grow.

For teachers, Adaptive Reader provides a valuable tool to support differentiated instruction. You can assign the same novel to your entire class while ensuring each student reads a version that aligns with their reading level. This allows all students to participate in class discussions and activities, fostering a more inclusive learning environment.

For parents, Adaptive Reader offers a supportive tool to encourage your children's reading journey. As your child progresses through the different levels of a novel, they'll not only enhance their reading skills but also develop a deeper love for literature.

READING ACROSS MULTIPLE EDITIONS

All of our leveled novels include passage markers that correspond to the same content across every one of our editions. This means that passage '62' in our silver edition contains the same themes and plot elements as passage '62' in our original edition.

For teachers, this means that you can say "let's look at passage 35 together. What is the author trying to tell us here?" and all of your students will be reading the same content — but with vocabulary and syntax that's adapted to their reading level.

Our online reading tool, available at www.adaptivereader.com, gives students and teachers free access to the original text with passage markers. We encourage teachers to include close readings of the original text as part of their coursework, giving all students exposure to the rich original syntax and language of these exceptional authors.

THE POWER OF LITERATURE

At Adaptive Reader, we are committed to helping everyone experience the power of literature. So whether you're a student diving into a classic novel, a teacher looking for flexible resources, or a parent seeking ways to support your child's literacy, Adaptive Reader is here for you.

We invite you to embark on this exciting literary journey with us. Enjoy the world of stories, characters, and ideas that await you in our collection of leveled novels. Happy reading!

RAPPACCINI'S DAUGHTER

A YOUNG MAN named Giovanni Guasconti traveled a long time ago from southern Italy to study at the University of Padua. Giovanni didn't have much money, so he rented a small, dark room in an old building that once belonged to a rich family. This family was long gone, but their symbol was still on the building's entrance.

Giovanni remembered a famous poem from his country that talked about someone from this family. This person was said to suffer forever in a terrible place called Inferno. Thinking of these sad stories and being away from home for the first time made Giovanni feel lonely. He sighed heavily as he looked around his empty and plain room.

"Goodness, sir!" said old Dame Lisabetta, who liked Giovanni because he was very handsome. She tried to make the room nicer for him and said, "Why are you so sad? Is this old place making you unhappy? For heaven's sake, look out the window! You'll see sunshine just as bright as it is back in Naples."

Giovanni did as the old woman suggested but didn't think the sunshine in Padua was as bright as it was in southern Italy. Still, the sunlight fell on a garden below his window, filled with many well-cared-for plants.

"Does this garden belong to the house?" Giovanni asked.

"Heaven forbid, signor! No, that garden is taken care of by Signor Giacomo Rappaccini, the famous doctor you might have heard about, even in Naples," answered old Lisabetta. "They say he makes powerful medicines from these plants. Sometimes, you can see him working in the garden, and maybe even his daughter, picking the strange flowers."

After tidying up the room as best as she could, the old woman wished Giovanni well and left.

Giovanni had nothing else to do, so he looked down at the garden below his window. It seemed like one of those old plant gardens that had been in Padua for a long time. Maybe it once belonged to a rich family because there was an old, broken marble fountain in the center. The fountain still had water flowing and sparkling in the sunlight, making a happy bubbling sound that reached Giovanni's window.

The water seemed to sing a timeless song, not caring about the changes around it. Plants with big leaves and bright flowers grew around the pool where the water collected. One particular bush, placed in a marble pot in the middle of the pool, had many purple flowers. These flowers were so rich and shiny that they looked like jewels and made the whole garden bright, even without sunlight.

The garden was full of plants and herbs, each cared for with great attention. Some plants were in fancy carved pots, while others were in simple garden ones. Some plants crawled along the ground like snakes, and others climbed up anything they could find.

One plant wrapped itself around a statue of Vertumnus, covering it with beautiful leaves that looked like a sculptor had arranged them.

As Giovanni watched from his window, he heard rustling behind the leaves. He saw a person working in the garden. It wasn't an ordinary gardener but a tall, thin, sickly-looking man, dressed in black like a scholar.

The man had gray hair and a thin beard, with a serious face that showed he was very smart, but he didn't seem like a warm or friendly person.

The scientist examined each plant carefully as he walked. He seemed to be trying to understand why the leaves and flowers looked the way they did.

But even though he knew a lot about the plants, he didn't get too close. He was very careful not to touch them or breathe in their smells. This made Giovanni feel uneasy because the man acted like the plants were dangerous animals or something evil that could harm him.

It was strange for Giovanni to see someone so scared while working in a garden. Gardening is usually a peaceful and safe activity that people have enjoyed for a long time. Was this garden special, like the Garden of Eden? And was this man, who saw danger in the plants he grew, like Adam?

The gardener wore thick gloves to protect his hands when he trimmed the plants and removed dead leaves. These gloves were part of his protection.

During his walk in the garden, the scientist reached a beautiful plant with purple flowers near a marble fountain. He put a mask over his mouth and nose, as if the plant might be dangerous. Still feeling unsafe, he stepped back, removed the mask, and shouted in a weak voice, "Beatrice! Beatrice!"

"Here I am, father. What do you need?" replied a strong and youthful voice from a nearby house. The voice made Giovanni think of rich colors and sweet smells.

"Yes, Beatrice," the scientist said, "I need your help."

A young girl soon appeared. She was dressed beautifully, like the bright flowers around her. She looked healthy and full of life.

Giovanni stared into the garden, and his imagination ran wild. He thought of the young woman he saw as another flower in the garden, more beautiful than the rest, but he felt she should only be touched with a glove and approached with a mask. As Beatrice walked down the garden path, Giovanni noticed she touched and smelled the plants that her father had carefully avoided.

"Beatrice," her father said, "look how many tasks need to be done for our special plant. I am too weak and might get hurt if I go too close. You will have to take care of it from now on."

"I will gladly do it!" Beatrice replied in her beautiful voice, reaching out to the plant. "Yes, my beautiful plant, it will be my job to take care of you. You will thank me with your lovely smell, which is like the breath of life to me."

Then, with great care, Beatrice tended to the plant as if it was her sister. Giovanni watched from his window, wondering if he was seeing a girl caring for her favorite flower or a sister showing love to another. Soon, the scene ended.

Dr. Rappaccini had either finished his work or noticed Giovanni watching. He took Beatrice by the arm and left the garden. As night came, strange smells rose from the plants, and Giovanni shut his window. He went to bed and dreamed of a lovely flower and a beautiful girl. They seemed different but also the same, and both had something mysterious about them.

In the bright light of morning, Giovanni felt clearer. He opened his window and looked down at the garden that seemed so full of mysteries in his dream.

He was surprised to see how normal everything looked in the sunlight. The drops of dew on the leaves and flowers sparkled brightly, making the garden look even more beautiful. Giovanni was happy that he could see such a lovely garden in the middle of the city.

He thought the garden would help him stay connected with nature. Neither Dr. Rappaccini nor his daughter was in the garden, so Giovanni couldn't figure out if they were really as strange as he had imagined. He decided to think more reasonably about the whole thing.

Later that day, he visited Signor Pietro Baglioni, a well-known professor of medicine at the university. Giovanni had a letter to introduce himself. The professor was an older man who seemed friendly and cheerful.

Giovanni stayed for dinner, and Professor Baglioni was very friendly and talkative, especially after having some wine. Giovanni thought it was natural to talk about Dr. Rappaccini since they were both doctors in the same city. But Professor Baglioni's reaction wasn't as friendly as Giovanni had expected.

"As a teacher of medicine," said Professor Baglioni, answering Giovanni's question, "I should praise Dr. Rappaccini for his skills. However, as a responsible person, I must warn you, Signor Giovanni, the son of an old friend, not to have any wrong ideas about him, because he might have control over your future health.

Dr. Rappaccini is very knowledgeable, maybe the best in Padua or even all of Italy. But there are some serious concerns about his character as a doctor."

"What are those concerns?" asked Giovanni.

"Why is my friend Giovanni so curious about doctors? Does he have a sickness?" asked the professor with a smile. "As for Rappaccini, I know him well. People say he cares more about science than about people. His patients are just experiments to him. He would risk human lives, even his own, just to learn a little more."

"He sounds like a scary man," said Giovanni, thinking about how cold and serious Rappaccini seemed. "But isn't it good to love science so much?"

"God forbid," replied the professor quickly. "Not unless they have better ideas about medicine than Rappaccini. He believes that the best medicines come from poisonous plants.

He grows these plants himself and has even made new, more dangerous ones. It's true that Dr. Rappaccini causes less harm than he could with such poisons."

Now and then, Dr. Rappaccini has done some amazing cures, but

I think he's just lucky. When he fails, it's his own fault, and he should be blamed for that," said Professor Baglioni.

Giovanni didn't know there was a long-standing rivalry between Baglioni and Dr. Rappaccini, and that Rappaccini was usually seen as the better doctor. If you want to judge for yourself, there are old books at the University of Padua about both of them.

"I don't know, wise professor," Giovanni said after thinking about Rappaccini's love for science. "I don't know how much he loves his work, but he surely loves one thing more. He has a daughter."

"Aha!" laughed the professor. "So now we know your secret, Giovanni. You have heard about his daughter. All the young men in Padua are crazy about her, though not many have actually seen her."

"I don't know much about Signora Beatrice, except that her father, Dr. Rappaccini, has taught her a lot about science. Even though she's young and beautiful, people say she's smart enough to be a professor. Maybe she will take my place one day! There are other silly rumors too, but they aren't worth mentioning. Now, Giovanni, finish your drink."

Giovanni left feeling a bit dizzy from the wine. As he walked home, he thought about Dr. Rappaccini and Beatrice. He stopped at a flower shop and bought some fresh flowers.

When he got to his room, he sat by the window where he could see the garden without being seen. The garden was quiet. Strange plants were sunbathing and gently nodding to each other, as if they were friends.

In the middle of the garden, near a broken fountain, was a big, beautiful plant with purple flowers. The flowers sparkled in the sun and reflected in the water, making the pool look colorful. At first, the garden looked empty."

After Giovanni returned to his room, he looked out the window into the garden. He saw a girl appear from an old carved doorway. She walked between the rows of plants, smelling their sweet scents as if she loved them.

When Giovanni saw Beatrice again, he was amazed. She was even more beautiful than he remembered. Her face shone in the sunlight, making the shadows around her seem brighter. Giovanni noticed her simple and kind expression and wondered who she really was.

Beatrice's dress matched the colorful flowers of a stunning plant by the fountain. She went up to the plant, opened her arms wide, and hugged it. Her face and hair mingled with the leaves and flowers, almost becoming part of the plant.

"Give me your breath, sister," said Beatrice. "I feel weak with the regular air. And let me have this flower of yours, which I gently take from the stem and place near my heart."

With these words, Beatrice, the beautiful daughter of Rappaccini, picked one of the brightest flowers from the bush and was about to pin it to her dress. But then, a strange thing happened.

A small orange-colored lizard was crawling along the path near Beatrice's feet. Giovanni thought he saw a drop of sap from the flower fall on the lizard's head. For a moment, the lizard twisted in pain and then stopped moving.

Beatrice saw this strange event and made the sign of the cross, sadly but not surprised. She still pinned the flower to her dress, where it sparkled like a jewel, adding a special charm that nothing else could give. But Giovanni, watching from his window, leaned forward, then pulled back, whispering and trembling.

"Am I dreaming? Is this real?" he wondered. "Is she beautiful or something scary?"

Beatrice wandered through the garden, coming closer to Giovanni's window. He leaned out to see her better because he was very curious.

Just then, a pretty butterfly flew over the garden wall. It might have flown around the city but found no flowers until it smelled the sweet scents from Dr. Rappaccini's plants. The butterfly didn't land on the flowers but seemed interested in Beatrice and flew around her head.

Giovanni couldn't believe his eyes. He thought he saw the butterfly get weak and fall at Beatrice's feet. Its bright wings stopped moving, and it looked dead. He didn't know why this happened, but he guessed it might be because of her breath. Beatrice saw the dead butterfly, made a sign with her hand, and sighed sadly.

Giovanni moved suddenly, and Beatrice noticed him at the window. She saw his handsome face with its golden curls looking down at her. Without thinking much, Giovanni threw down a bunch of flowers he was holding.

"Signora," he said, "these flowers are fresh and pure. Please wear them for me, Giovanni Guasconti."

"Thank you, signor," Beatrice replied, her voice sounding like lovely music. She smiled, half like a child and half like a woman. "I accept your gift but cannot give you this special purple flower back because it won't reach you. So you must be happy with my thanks."

She picked up the flowers from the ground. Feeling shy for talking to a stranger, she quickly went back to her house through the garden. To Giovanni, it seemed like his beautiful flowers were already starting to wilt in her hands as she disappeared. But he knew it was just his imagination; there was no way to tell if the flowers were wilting from such a distance.

For many days after what happened, Giovanni stayed away from the window that looked into Dr. Rappaccini's garden. He worried that seeing it would be bad for him. He felt strange, like he had gotten involved with something powerful and mysterious because he had talked to Beatrice.

If he really wanted to stay safe, the smartest thing would have been to leave his apartment and Padua completely. Another good idea would have been to look at Beatrice in the daytime when things seemed normal. But staying close by and not looking at her was probably the worst choice because it let his imagination go wild.

Giovanni didn't have a very deep heart, but he had a wild imagination and a passionate nature. Whether or not Beatrice was truly dangerous like the flowers in the garden, she had certainly cast a strong and strange influence over him.

It wasn't just love, even though her beauty drove him crazy; nor was it pure fear, even though he thought she might have dangerous powers. It was a mix of both emotions that confused him, making him feel both warm and cold inside.

Giovanni didn't know what to fear or what to hope for, but these feelings fought inside him constantly. Sometimes he felt hopeful, and other times he was filled with dread. Having simple, clear emotions would have been better, but his mixed feelings were like a storm in his heart.

To calm down, Giovanni often took fast walks through the streets of Padua, trying to match his steps to his racing thoughts. One day, during one of these walks, he suddenly stopped. A large, friendly man had recognized him and grabbed his arm, out of breath from catching up.

"Giovanni! Wait, my friend!" the man called out. "Have you forgotten me? You look much changed, so I wouldn't be surprised."

It was Professor Baglioni. Giovanni had been avoiding him because he was afraid the professor might guess his secrets. Trying to act normal, Giovanni spoke as if in a daze.

"Yes, I am Giovanni Guasconti. You are Professor Baglioni. Now let me go!"

"Not so fast, Giovanni," said the professor, smiling but looking closely at him. "I knew your father well. How can I let his son walk past me like a stranger? We must talk."

"Hurry up, please, Professor," replied Giovanni impatiently. "Can't you see I'm in a rush?"

As they spoke, a man in black walked slowly down the street. He looked sick and weak, but his sharp eyes made him seem very intelligent.

As he walked by, the man gave Baglioni a quick nod but stared at Giovanni in a way that felt like he was studying him closely. The look was curious but distant.

"That's Dr. Rappaccini," whispered Baglioni after the man passed. "Has he ever seen you before?"

"I don't think so," Giovanni replied, surprised by the name.

"He has seen you! I'm sure of it!" Baglioni said urgently. "This man studies people like he studies plants and animals. He's watching you closely, just like he watches a flower or a butterfly in his experiments. Giovanni, I believe you're part of one of Rappaccini's experiments!"

"Are you trying to scare me?" Giovanni shouted, upset. "This doesn't make sense!"

"Calm down," said Baglioni calmly. "I'm telling you, Rappaccini is very interested in you. Be careful, Giovanni! And what about Signora Beatrice? How is she involved in this mystery?"

Giovanni couldn't stand Professor Baglioni's nagging anymore, so he ran off before the professor could grab his arm. Baglioni watched him go, shaking his head.

"This can't happen," Baglioni thought to himself. "Giovanni is my old friend's son, and I must protect him from harm. Rappaccini can't just use him for his weird experiments. And his daughter? I need to figure out what's going on!"

Giovanni took a long way around and finally got to his home. At the door, he was greeted by old Lisabetta, who eagerly tried to get his attention. Giovanni, deep in thought, didn't notice her smile. She grabbed his cloak and whispered, "Signor, listen! There is a secret way into the garden!"

"What did you say?" Giovanni asked, turning around quickly. "A secret way into Dr. Rappaccini's garden?"

"Hush, not so loud!" whispered Lisabetta, covering his mouth with her hand. "Yes, into the doctor's garden where you can see all his special plants. Many young men in Padua would pay gold to see those flowers."

Giovanni gave her a gold coin.

"Show me the way," he said.

He remembered his chat with Professor Baglioni and wondered if this was part of a plan involving Dr. Rappaccini. But the thought of seeing Beatrice made it impossible for Giovanni to resist.

24 It didn't matter if she was an angel or a demon; Giovanni felt he had to be near her. He was being pulled towards something he couldn't predict. Then, suddenly, he felt unsure. Was his strong interest real, or just in his imagination? Was he just a young man dreaming, not truly in love?

He stopped, thought about turning back, but continued. His old guide led him through some hidden pathways and finally opened a door. Giovanni could hear leaves rustling and see sunlight shining through them. He stepped through, pushing past a plant, and found himself standing under his own window in Dr. Rappaccini's garden.

Sometimes, when our wildest dreams come true, we feel surprisingly calm. Life loves to surprise us this way.

25 Giovanni had been eager to meet Beatrice in the garden. He had imagined this moment many times, thinking about how beautiful she was and what secrets she might reveal to him.

But now that he was actually in the garden, he felt surprisingly calm. He looked around to see if Beatrice or her father were there, but realized he was alone. He started looking closely at the plants.

The plants looked strange to him. They were very colorful and seemed almost too wild, like they didn't belong in a normal garden. Giovanni thought they seemed a bit scary, like something magical or unusual was hiding there.

26 Several of the plants looked strange and fake, as if they were made by mixing different kinds together, creating something unnatural. These plants seemed like they were made by people, not by nature, and they had a strange and dangerous beauty. They were probably the result of experiments trying to combine different plants, turning lovely flowers into something odd and scary.

Giovanni only recognized two or three types of plants, and he knew those were poisonous. While he was thinking about this, he heard the sound of a dress and saw Beatrice coming through a fancy gate.

Giovanni wasn't sure how to act; he didn't know if he should apologize for being in the garden or pretend he had permission from Dr. Rappaccini or Beatrice to be there. But Beatrice's kind and happy look made him feel comfortable, even though he still didn't know how he got into the garden. She walked gracefully down the path and met him by the broken fountain, surprised but happy to see him.

"Do you like flowers, signor?" Beatrice asked with a smile, referring to the bouquet he had thrown from the window. "It makes sense that my father's collection would attract you. If he were here, he could tell you many interesting things about these plants, since he has spent his life studying them. This garden is his world."

"And you, lady," Giovanni said, "if rumors are true, you also know a lot about these beautiful flowers and their smells. Would you teach me? I would learn better from you than even from Signor Rappaccini."

"Are there such silly rumors?" Beatrice laughed. "Do people say I know as much as my father about plants? What a joke! No, even though I have grown up with these flowers, I only know their colors and smells. Sometimes I wish I didn't even know that much. There are many flowers here that I dislike. But please, signor, do not believe these stories about me. Only believe what you see with your own eyes."

"Do I have to believe everything I've seen with my own eyes?" Giovanni asked, feeling uneasy. "No, signora. Tell me to believe only what you say."

Beatrice seemed to understand. She blushed but looked straight into Giovanni's eyes.

"I ask you to do just that," she replied. "Forget what you think you've seen. Even if it seemed true, it might not be. But my words are always true. Believe them."

Beatrice's words glowed with sincerity, and Giovanni felt her truthfulness. Yet, he could smell a sweet fragrance around her, perhaps from the flowers. He wondered if it was Beatrice's breath making her words seem so rich and deep. A brief dizziness came over

Giovanni but quickly left. Looking into Beatrice's eyes, he felt all his doubts disappear.

Beatrice's serious mood disappeared. She became happy and talked with Giovanni, finding joy as if she were meeting someone new and exciting. Before, Beatrice had only known life in the garden.

She chatted about simple things like the sky and her garden and asked Giovanni about his city, home, friends, and family. Her questions showed she didn't know much about the outside world, and Giovanni answered kindly, just like he would to a younger person.

Beatrice shared her thoughts, and they were bright and lively, like sparkling jewels. Giovanni marveled at how he was walking and talking with Beatrice, the girl he once thought of with fear. Now, she seemed so normal and friendly, just like any other girl.

But these thoughts did not last long; Beatrice's true nature was too strong to ignore.

As they wandered through the garden, they reached an old fountain next to a beautiful plant with bright, glowing flowers. The plant's smell was the same as Beatrice's breath but much stronger. When Beatrice saw it, she clutched her chest as if in sudden pain.

"For the first time, I had forgotten you," she whispered to the plant.

"I remember, signora," Giovanni said, "you promised me a flower for the bouquet I gave you. May I take one now as a memory of our meeting?"

He reached out toward the plant, but Beatrice quickly stopped him, crying out in fear. She pulled his hand back with surprising strength. Giovanni felt a shiver from her touch.

"Don't touch it!" she cried. "Not for your life! It is deadly!"

Then, hiding her face, she ran away from him and disappeared through the decorated doorway. Giovanni watched her go and saw Dr. Rappaccini, thin and serious, standing in the shadows of the entrance.

When Giovanni was alone in his room, he couldn't stop thinking about Beatrice. He remembered her with all the magic he had felt since the first time he saw her. She seemed so kind and gentle, and he believed she was worthy of love.

The strange things he had noticed about her before now seemed like they made her even more special. What had once seemed scary now seemed beautiful. Anything that couldn't be made pretty just faded away from his thoughts.

Giovanni stayed awake all night, dreaming about the beautiful garden and Beatrice. As the sun came up, its light woke him up, and he felt a burning pain in his right hand—the same hand Beatrice had held when he almost picked one of the shiny flowers. Looking at his hand, he saw a purple mark like tiny fingers and a small thumb on his wrist.

Love can be strong, even if it's just in your imagination. Giovanni wrapped his hand with a cloth and wondered what had hurt him. But soon, he forgot the pain and started thinking about Beatrice again.

After their first meeting, Giovanni saw Beatrice again and again. He looked forward to their meetings every day. Their time together in the garden became the most important part of his life, and he thought about it all the time.

Beatrice, Dr. Rappaccini's daughter, waited for Giovanni every day, watching for him with as much trust as if they had been friends since they were little. If Giovanni didn't arrive on time, Beatrice would stand under his window and call out to him, "Giovanni! Giovanni! Why are you late? Come down!" Giovanni would quickly go to the garden full of dangerous flowers.

Even though they spent a lot of time together, Beatrice was always a little distant. Giovanni respected this and never thought of breaking that distance.

They loved each other deeply. They showed their love through their eyes and their words, feeling that their love was too special to be spoken aloud. But they had never kissed, held hands, or shared any small touch that love often includes.

Giovanni had never touched even a single strand of Beatrice's hair. Her clothes had never even brushed against him. When Giovanni seemed like he might get too close, Beatrice would look so sad and serious, like a wall between them. She didn't need to say a word for Giovanni to step back.

During those moments, Giovanni felt terrible suspicions rise within him, making his love feel weak and doubtful. But when Beatrice's face brightened again, she changed from being a mysterious girl he was scared of into the sweet girl he felt he truly knew.

A long time had passed since Giovanni last saw Professor Baglioni. One morning, to his surprise, the professor visited him. Giovanni hadn't thought about him for weeks and didn't miss him. He didn't want anyone around unless they understood his feelings perfectly. He knew the professor wouldn't.

The visitor talked casually for a while about the city's news and the university, and then brought up another topic.

"I was reading an old book," he said, "and found a story that really interested me. Maybe you know it. It's about an Indian prince who gave a beautiful woman to Alexander the Great as a gift. She was as lovely as the morning and as colorful as the evening sky. But what made her special was the sweet smell of her breath, sweeter than a garden full of flowers. Alexander, being a young king, fell in love with her at first sight. But a wise doctor who was there found out an awful secret about her."

"And what was that?" asked Giovanni, looking away to avoid the professor's eyes.

"The doctor found out," Baglioni said seriously, "that this beautiful woman had been given poisons her whole life, so she had become the most dangerous poison herself. Her breath was poisonous, and her love would bring death. Isn't that an amazing story?"

"That's a silly tale," Giovanni said, jumping up from his chair. "I wonder how you find time to read such nonsense with your important work?"

"By the way," said the professor, looking around nervously, "what is that strange smell in your room? Is it from your gloves? It's faint but interesting, yet it feels like it might make me sick if I smell it too long. It's like the scent of a flower, but I don't see any flowers here."

"There aren't any flowers," replied Giovanni, who had turned pale as the professor spoke. "I think the smell you notice is just your imagination. Sometimes, we can remember a smell so well that it feels like it's real, even when it isn't."

"Maybe," said Baglioni, "but my mind doesn't usually play tricks on me like that. If I were to imagine a smell, it would be one I often encounter at work, like the strong scent of medicine. I've heard that Dr. Rappaccini uses very fragrant things in his mixtures. And his daughter, Beatrice, might make medicines that smell sweet, but it would be dangerous to drink them!"

Giovanni looked very upset. The way the professor spoke about Rappaccini's daughter hurt him deeply, but it also made him think of all the doubts he had about her. These doubts felt like scary monsters in his mind. Still, Giovanni tried hard to stay calm and to trust her.

"Professor," he said, "you were my father's friend and maybe you want to help me too. I want to respect you, but please understand that we cannot talk about Signora Beatrice. You don't know her, so your words about her are unfair and hurtful."

"Giovanni, my poor boy," said the professor sadly, "I know more about this girl than you do. I must tell you the truth about her and her father, Rappaccini. They use strange and dangerous science, and Beatrice is part of it. She's as dangerous as she is beautiful. Listen to me, even if it makes you angry, because this is important."

Giovanni groaned and covered his face with his hands.

"Her father," continued Professor Baglioni, "didn't care about the danger he put his daughter in. He is obsessed with his science experiments. What will happen to you, Giovanni? You might be part of one of his tests. It could end badly for you, maybe even worse than you can imagine. Rappaccini will stop at nothing for his experiments."

"It feels like a bad dream," Giovanni whispered to himself.

"But don't worry," said the professor. "There is still hope. Maybe we can help Beatrice become normal again, away from her father's crazy experiments. Look at this small silver vase. It was made by a famous artist and would be a perfect gift. But its liquid is even more special.

One sip of it can stop the strongest poisons. I'm sure it will work against Rappaccini's poisons too. Give this vase to Beatrice, and let's hope for the best."

Baglioni left a small silver vial on the table as he walked away, hoping his words would make Giovanni think.

"We will stop Rappaccini yet," Baglioni muttered to himself as he went downstairs. "But I must admit, he is a brilliant man. Still, his bad methods should not be accepted by good doctors."

Giovanni had always had some doubts about Beatrice, wondering if she was more than she seemed. But she always appeared to be kind and loving, making Professor Baglioni's warnings seem hard to believe.

It was true, Giovanni remembered that strange things happened when he first met Beatrice. Flowers wilted in her hand, and insects died around her just from her breath. But seeing how good she was made Giovanni think these were just mistakes, not real facts.

There are things that are truer and more real than what we can see and touch. Giovanni believed in Beatrice not just because of what he saw, but because he felt she was special. However, now he started to doubt her. His early excitement started to fade, and he began to question Beatrice.

He didn't stop caring about her; he just didn't trust her completely. Giovanni decided he needed a test to find out if she really had strange powers. He thought maybe his eyes tricked him before when he saw the lizard, insect, and flowers. But if he saw a healthy flower die in her hand up close, he would know for sure.

With this plan in mind, he quickly went to the flower shop and bought a fresh bouquet still covered with morning dew-drops.

It was time for Giovanni to meet Beatrice in the garden. Before going down, Giovanni looked at himself in the mirror. He was proud of how handsome he looked, but it also showed he might be a bit shallow. He admired his face, thinking he looked more lively and healthy than ever before.

"At least," he thought, "her poison hasn't gotten to me. I'm not like those flowers that die in her hands."

He then looked at the bouquet he had been holding. Suddenly, a fear went through him. The fresh flowers were starting to droop and wilt. Giovanni's face turned as pale as a ghost. He stood still, staring at his reflection with horror.

Giovanni thought about what Professor Baglioni had said about a strange smell in the room. Could it be poison coming from his own breath? This idea scared him. He noticed a spider making a web in the corner of the room. Giovanni leaned closer and breathed on the spider.

The spider stopped moving. The web shook as if the spider was frightened. Giovanni breathed on it again, even harder this time, with a mix of fear and anger. The spider twitched and then fell dead.

"Oh no!" Giovanni whispered to himself. "Is my breath so poisonous that it can kill a spider?"

Just then, he heard a sweet voice from the garden calling, "Giovanni! Giovanni! You're late! Come down!"

"Yes," Giovanni mumbled. "She's the only one my breath doesn't harm. I wish it did!"

He hurried downstairs and soon stood in front of Beatrice, looking into her bright and loving eyes.

A moment ago, Giovanni had been very angry and upset. He had almost wished he could hurt Beatrice just by looking at her. But when she was really there, he remembered the good things about her. She had made him feel calm and peaceful many times. If Giovanni could have understood these feelings, he would have known that the bad things he thought about her were not true. The real Beatrice was kind and good.

Even though he could not fully believe in her goodness, her presence still had a strong effect on him. Giovanni's anger faded, and he felt very sad instead. Beatrice could sense the sadness and the distance between them.

They walked together without speaking until they reached a marble fountain with a pool of water. In the middle of the pool was a plant with beautiful flowers. Giovanni was worried about how much he liked the smell of the flowers.

"Beatrice," he asked suddenly, "where did this plant come from?"

"My father made it," answered Beatrice simply.

"Made it? How?" asked Giovanni.

"He knows many secrets of nature," Beatrice replied. "When I was born, this plant grew from the ground because of his science. It's like his other child. Don't get closer!" She saw Giovanni moving towards the shrub with alarm.

"It's more dangerous than you think. But I, Giovanni, I grew up with this plant. It's like my sister, and I loved it. Sadly, didn't you guess? There's something terrible about it."

Giovanni frowned, making Beatrice stop and shake. But she trusted him and continued.

"There was a curse, because of my father's science, that kept me away from people. Until Heaven sent you, Giovanni, I was so lonely!"

"Was it a tough curse?" asked Giovanni.

"Only now do I know how hard it was," she replied softly. "Yes, but my heart was numb and quiet."

Giovanni's anger exploded like a lightning bolt from a storm.

"You're cursed!" shouted Giovanni angrily. "You were lonely and dragged me into your awful world, too!"

"Giovanni," said Beatrice, her eyes wide with surprise. She couldn't understand his harsh words.

"Yes, you poisonous thing!" Giovanni yelled. "You ruined my life! You filled me with poison and made me as terrible as you! Let's kiss and end this together if we're so deadly!"

"What has happened to me?" Beatrice whispered, her heart aching. "Help me, I'm just a sad, broken girl."

"You pray?" Giovanni sneered. "Your prayers are like poison. Let's go to church and dip our fingers in holy water; we'll spread death wherever we go! Let's make the sign of the cross; it will curse everything around us!"

"Giovanni," said Beatrice softly, feeling very sad, "Why do you speak to me like this? I know you think I am horrible. But you can just leave this garden and forget about me."

"Don't you understand?" Giovanni said, frowning at her. "Look at what your father's garden has done to me."

A bunch of summer insects flew around Giovanni's head, attracted by the flowers' smell. Giovanni blew on them, and many of the bugs fell to the ground, dead. He looked at Beatrice with a bitter smile.

"I see it! I see it!" cried Beatrice. "It's my father's terrible science! No, Giovanni, it wasn't me! Never! I just wanted to love you and spend some time with you. But my father has connected us in this awful way. Yes, hate me, push me away, even kill me! But it wasn't me. Never would I have done this."

Giovanni was no longer angry. He felt sad and realized how closely connected they were. They stood alone together, even if there were many people around them.

Shouldn't the big, lonely world around them bring Giovanni and Beatrice closer together? If they were mean to each other, who would be kind to them? Giovanni hoped he could go back to a normal life and lead Beatrice, the better Beatrice, with him too. But how could he think of being happy together when he had hurt Beatrice's feelings so badly with his cruel words? There was no real hope for that.

Beatrice would have to move on with her broken heart, and maybe one day she would find peace and happiness.

But Giovanni didn't know this for sure.

"Dear Beatrice," Giovanni said, walking towards her. She moved away from him, but now for a different reason. "Dearest Beatrice, we are not doomed yet. Look! There's a special medicine, made from blessed herbs, that a wise doctor has told me about. It's the opposite of what your father used to harm us. Shall we drink it together and be free from the bad things?”

49 "Give it to me!” said Beatrice as she reached out for the little silver vial Giovanni held. "I'll drink it, but you wait and see what happens,” she added.

Beatrice put the antidote to her lips just as Rappaccini came out and walked towards them. He had a proud look on his face, like someone who had finally completed a great work of art.

He stopped, stood tall, and spread his hands out like he was giving a blessing, but those were the same hands that had poisoned their lives. Giovanni shook with fear, and Beatrice pressed her hand on her heart, scared.

"My daughter,” said Rappaccini, "you are no longer alone. Pick a flower from your sister plant and give it to Giovanni. It won't harm him now. My science has made him like you, different from normal people. Now, go on through the world, being very special to each other but feared by everyone else.”

50 "Father,” said Beatrice weakly, keeping her hand on her heart, "why did you put this horrible curse on me?”

"Horrible?” replied Rappaccini. "What are you talking about, silly girl? Do you think it's horrible to have amazing powers that no one can fight against? Is it bad to be able to defeat anyone with a breath or to be as terrifying as you are beautiful? Would you rather be a weak woman, exposed to all dangers and unable to fight back?”

"I wanted to be loved, not feared,” whispered Beatrice, sinking to the ground. "But now it doesn't matter. I'm leaving, father, where the evil you put in me will fade away like the scent of these poisonous flowers. Goodbye, Giovanni! Your hateful words hurt my heart, but they will disappear, too, as I rise. Oh, wasn't there more poison in you than in me?”

For Beatrice—whose body had been so changed by Rappaccini's experiments—the poison had become her life, and the antidote was killing her. And so, the poor victim of her father's cleverness and twisted wisdom, died there at the feet of her father and Giovanni.

51   At that moment, Professor Baglioni looked out the window. He shouted with a mix of triumph and horror to the shocked scientist, "Rappaccini! Rappaccini! Is this the result of your experiment?"